Rupert and the Stepping Stones

EGMONT

Rupert Bear had arranged to meet his friends at the treehouse. They were going to explore the other side of Nutwood Forest.

"I'm off to meet the others," Rupert called out to his mum. "See you later!"

He jumped into his pedal car and sped off.

When Rupert approached the treehouse, his friends were looking glum.

"What's wrong?" he asked.

"Ask Raggety," grumbled Bill Badger.

Rupert Bear looked over at Raggety. "Don't you want to come exploring with us?" Rupert asked him.

Raggety shook his head. "Funny magic other side of forest," he said. "Raggety stay here, please. Thank you."

But Rupert knew how to change his mind. "You can ride in my pedal car if you come with us," he smiled.

When Raggety looked over at Rupert's car, his face lit up. "OK!" he said, jumping in.

The friends set off, and eventually came to a clearing on the other side of the forest. There were seven stones on the ground in a circle.

Rupert Bear and Ping Pong ran over to take a closer look. When Rupert stepped on one of the stones, it lit up and played a note!

"Let me try," said Ping Pong, jumping on another stone. It made a different sound from Rupert's.

Ming and Raggety were the only ones not joining in. Ming climbed into Rupert's car for a nap, but Raggety was looking worried. "Funny magic," he kept saying.

Bill Badger and Edward Trunk jumped on different stones. Bill's made a high note. Edward's made a low note. The friends began to jump from stone to stone, playing different tunes.

"Come on, Raggety," called Rupert. "Join in. We can make up a tune together."

Raggety came a little closer.

"Raggety not sure . . ." he said. But it did look fun!

Finally, he plucked up the courage. He jumped on a stone to complete the friends' tune.

Suddenly, there was a loud rumbling sound and a swirl of purple smoke began to rise from the middle of the stones.

"Funny magic . . . Raggety said!" cried Raggety, running away and hiding behind a tree.

A little genie appeared out of the purple smoke. He rubbed his eyes and grumbled about being woken up.

"Who are you?" asked Rupert Bear.

"I am the Genie of the Stepping Stones," said the little genie. "You called!"

The genie quickly noticed Rupert's car. "Ooooh!" he smiled. As he pointed at the car, bright sparkles of magic flew from his fingers and circled the car.

The genie's magic lifted Rupert's car high into the air. Ming yapped. She wanted to be on the ground!

Ping Pong threw some of her magic dust up into the air and chanted:

"Pedal car, up so high,

Come down now and do not fly!"

But the genie didn't want the fun to end. His magic sparkles made the car spin round and round, until Ming was dizzy.

"Oh, Rupert!" cried Ping Pong. "What shall we do?"

"Raggety, can you help?" Rupert Bear asked Raggety, who was peeking out from behind his tree.

Raggety blew a magic wind to bring the car gently back down.

But the genie wasn't happy. He sent out his sparkles again and the car flew off, high above the trees.

"Don't worry, Ming," yelled Ping Pong, jumping on her tricycle. "I'm coming!"

And Ping Pong raced off after the car.

The friends looked at the genie. He was playing around the Stepping Stones.

He didn't understand all the trouble he had caused.

"**H**ow are we going to stop him?" whispered Bill Badger.

"We'll have to try and send him back home," replied Rupert.

"You can't," said the genie. "Not unless you play the same tune that woke me up!"

So *that* was the way to stop the genie!

But there was one problem. No one could remember the tune!

The genie teased the friends, as they jumped from stone to stone. "You'll never guess!" he said, hopping around wildly.

Bill Badger tried, and so did Edward Trunk. They almost had the tune, but it still wasn't quite right.

Bill got out his pocket telescope to see where Ming was.

"Rupert! Look!" he called.

23

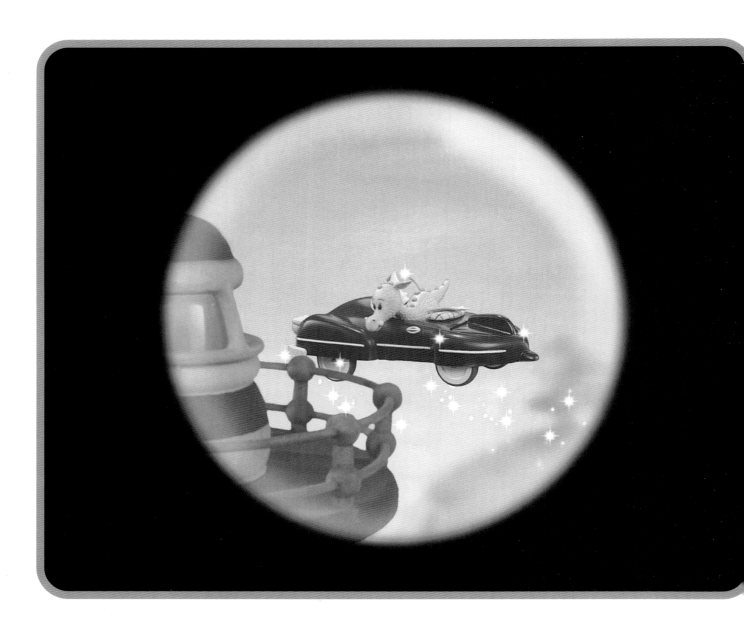

Through the telescope, Bill and Rupert could see the flying car. It was heading out towards Rocky Bay! If the car came down now, Ming might land in the sea!

Ping Pong was still chasing after the car on her tricycle. She came to a halt at the base of the Rocky Bay Lighthouse. She couldn't go any further.

"**H**ee, hee!" chuckled the genie, who was still leaping around. "Look, I can jump the highest!" But he missed his footing and fell with a bump on the ground.

Suddenly, the little genie began to cry. "I want my dad!" he wailed. "And I want to go home . . . NOW!"

"Don't worry," said Rupert Bear, comfortingly. "I'm sure we can get the tune right."

While Bill Badger looked through his telescope to see what was happening to Ming, Rupert jumped from stone to stone, but he couldn't remember the last note.

"Which one's next?" he wondered.

Raggety came to the rescue! He jumped on the right stone and finished the tune. They were all glad to see the swirl of purple smoke rising again. The genie's magic would soon be over.

Then Bill suddenly shouted, "Rupert, come and look! It's good news!"

Rupert Bear's car was landing gently beside Ping Pong. Ming was safe!

"I'm going home!" said the genie, happily. "Goodbye! Let's play again soon."

The friends watched the genie disappear. It was time for them to leave, too.

When Ping Pong and Ming had returned in Rupert's car, the friends set off for home.

On the way, they began to plan their next adventure. Ming, who was still a little dizzy, just hoped there would be no more spinning cars!

The End

EGMONT

We bring stories to life

First published in Great Britain 2008
by Egmont UK Limited
239 Kensington High Street, London W8 6SA
Rupert Bear ®. © Entertainment Rights Distribution Limited/
Express Newspapers 2008

ISBN 978 1 4052 4055 0
1 3 5 7 9 10 8 6 4 2
Printed in China